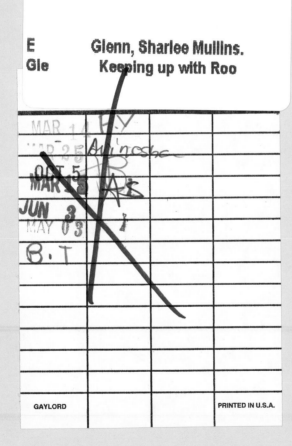

4.1/5

Keeping Up With Roo

GRACIE ME

SHARLEE GLENN

illustrated by

DAN ANDREASEN

G. P. Putnam's Sons · New York

In loving memory of my aunt Martha,
who taught me how to read.—S.G.

For my lovely wife, Sharon.—D.A.

Text copyright © 2004 by Sharlee Glenn
Illustrations copyright © 2004 by Dan Andreasen
All rights reserved. This book, or parts thereof, may not be
reproduced in any form without permission in writing from the publisher,
G. P. Putnam's Sons, a division of Penguin Young Readers Group,
345 Hudson Street, New York, NY 10014. G. P. Putnam's Sons, Reg. U.S. Pat. & Tm. Off.
The scanning, uploading and distribution of this book via the Internet or via any other
means without the permission of the publisher is illegal and punishable by law.
Please purchase only authorized electronic editions, and do not participate in or encourage
electronic piracy of copyrighted materials. Your support of the author's rights is appreciated.
Published simultaneously in Canada. Manufactured in China by South China Printing Co. Ltd.
Designed by Cecilia Yung and Gunta Alexander. Text set in Stempel Schneidler.
The art was done in graphite and oil paint on illustration board.
Library of Congress Cataloging-in-Publication Data
Glenn, Sharlee Mullins. Keeping up with Roo / Sharlee Glenn ; illustrated by Dan Andreasen.
p.   cm.   Summary: Gracie has always had a special bond with her aunt Roo, who is
mentally disabled, but that relationship starts to change when Gracie begins school.
[1. Interpersonal relations—Fiction. 2. People with mental disabilities—Fiction. 3. People with
disabilities—Fiction. 4. Aunts—Fiction. 5. Growth—Fiction.] I. Andreasen, Dan, ill. II. Title.
PZ7.G4855 Ke 2004   [E]—dc21   2002153864   ISBN 0-399-23480-2
10 9 8 7 6 5 4 3 2 1   First Impression

Gracie and Roo were best friends. It didn't matter that
Roo was almost as old as Mama and Gracie was only five.

When Gracie was a baby, Roo was the only one who could calm her when she got into a crying fit. Roo would take Gracie in her big arms and swoop around the room, singing: "Hang down your head, Tom Do-oo-ley. Hang down your head and cry. . . ." Gracie's little chin would quiver and unspilled tears would puddle in her eyes as she stared up at Roo.

Roo spent so much time holding the baby that Mama complained Gracie wouldn't know who was her mama and who was her aunt. But Mama smiled when she said it.

It was Roo who taught Gracie how to walk. One day shortly after Gracie's first birthday, Mama had to run into town. She asked Roo to baby-sit. When Mama got home, there was baby Gracie—arms flung toward the sky, little legs pumping—trying to keep up with her aunt, who was marching through the backyard to her own version of "Stars and Stripes Forever," scattering chickens in her wake.

Now that Gracie was five, she and Roo played together almost every day. As soon as her chores were done, Gracie would race over to the old farmhouse where Roo lived with Grandma and Grandpa. And what adventures they would have!

Running barefoot through the cornfield during rainstorms.

Stuffing themselves with tart red bull berries down by the river.

Tumbling down haystacks.

Once, they both fell off old Slicker when they tried to make him jump the corral fence. Roo sprained both wrists. Gracie landed on top of Roo and wasn't hurt at all.

They loved climbing trees and catching water skeeters and making whistles out of snake grass, but what they loved most was . . .

. . . playing school.

They set up their classroom under the willow tree in Grandma's yard, using a couple of old apple crates for desks. Roo was always the teacher. She would tap her crate with a willow switch and say, "Now, repeat after me: One plus one equals two, two plus two equals four, four plus four equals eight." That was as far as they could go with math. But Roo knew her ABC's
and how to read easy books.
Soon Gracie did too.

Then the summer was over and it was time for Gracie to start real school. Both Gracie and Roo cried.

"Why can't Roo come too?" Gracie sobbed.

"Your aunt Ruth is much too big for kindergarten," said Mama.

So off Gracie went on the huge yellow bus. Roo stood in the road and waved until the bus turned at the crossroads and disappeared.

Every day when Gracie got home, she and Roo would meet under the willow tree. When winter came, they moved inside to Roo's bedroom.

By the time Gracie was in second grade, she had taken over the willow switch and the teacher's desk. Gracie taught Roo how to count by fives, how to do dot-to-dots, how to spell "s-c-h-o-o-l," "k-i-t-t-e-n," "N-o-v-e-m-b-e-r." And she taught her that eight plus eight equals sixteen.

Roo spent her afternoons practicing her spelling and watching for the bus.

But then one day Gracie didn't want to have school with Roo
when she got home. She wanted Mama to drive her into town to
play at Sarah's house instead. And the next day she had to go
to piano lessons.

Every afternoon when Roo saw the old school bus rattle by,
she would rush out to the willow tree, sit at her apple crate, and
wait. Sometimes Gracie came and sometimes she didn't.

One day Sarah got to come to Gracie's house after school to play. Roo saw them get off the bus and ran down the lane to meet them.

"Who is that?" asked Sarah, grabbing Gracie and pointing at Roo.

Gracie looked up. Roo was wearing a pair of Grandpa's old overalls and a huge flowered shirt. She had been experimenting with hairstyles again and long green and purple ribbons streamed from a braid here, a pin curl there, as she bounced along and flapped her arms like an overgrown turkey trying to take flight.

"Oh, nobody," Gracie said hurriedly, and took Sarah's hand. "Come on, I'm starving."

Gracie glanced back once as she walked toward the house.
Roo had stopped in the middle of the road. The green and purple
ribbons fluttered gently around her legs. She just stood there,
like an abandoned May pole,
watching them go.

Gracie sliced ripe bananas onto graham crackers, then drizzled chocolate sauce over the top for an after-school snack.

"Umm. This is good," said Sarah between bites.

"My aunt Ruth made it up," said Gracie. Then she closed her eyes tight and shook her head, trying to erase the picture of Roo standing there alone on the road. Suddenly she didn't feel very hungry.

When Sarah had finished off the last graham cracker, they went into Gracie's room. Gracie showed Sarah her dolls, her rock collection, and the blue ribbon she'd won at last summer's 4-H fair.

"What's this?" asked Sarah, fingering a piece of brilliant painted glass hanging from a string in front of Gracie's window.

"Oh, that's just something my aunt Ruth gave me," said Gracie. "Let's go outside."

They explored the tree house, then went down by the creek.

"Look," said Gracie, plopping down on the bank and dangling her bare feet in the water. "If you pull out a piece of snake grass, tear it right here, then split the end, you can make a whistle."

"Neato!" said Sarah. "Where did you learn to do that?"

Gracie didn't answer. Blowing gently on her whistle, she watched the water swirl around her feet. Suddenly she stood up.

"Sarah," she said, "there's someone I want you to meet."

They found Roo inside Grandma's house, watching reruns on TV.
Roo's eyes opened wide when she saw them.

"Hurry up, Roo! We're late for school. It'll be even more fun
with three," said Gracie.

Roo beat them to the willow tree. She found the switch behind the teacher's desk and handed it to Gracie.

"No, Roo," said Gracie, handing it back. "You be the teacher this time."

Proudly Roo took the switch and tapped it on the apple crate. "Now, class, repeat after me," she said. "One plus one equals two, two plus two equals four, four plus four equals eight, eight plus eight . . ."